# Devi's Epiphany

## Chronicles of the Luminous Mysteries

Prakriti Sahu

**BLUEROSE PUBLISHERS**
India | U.K.

Copyright © Prakriti Sahu 2024

All rights reserved by author. No part of this publication may be reproduced, stored in a retrieval system or transmitted in any form or by any means, electronic, mechanical, photocopying, recording or otherwise, without the prior permission of the author. Although every precaution has been taken to verify the accuracy of the information contained herein, the publisher assumes no responsibility for any errors or omissions. No liability is assumed for damages that may result from the use of information contained within.

BlueRose Publishers takes no responsibility for any damages, losses, or liabilities that may arise from the use or misuse of the information, products, or services provided in this publication.

For permissions requests or inquiries regarding this publication, please contact:

BLUEROSE PUBLISHERS
www.BlueRoseONE.com
info@bluerosepublishers.com
+91 8882 898 898
+4407342408967

ISBN: 978-93-6452-831-3

Cover design: Shivani
Typesetting: Sagar

First Edition: October 2024

# Contents

Chapter 1
Prologue: The Awakening ............................................................ 1

Chapter 2
Dreamer's Vision ........................................................................ 5

Chapter 3
A Night of Revelation ................................................................ 14

Chapter 4
Vishwakarma's Legacy .............................................................. 21

Chapter 5
Echoes of Devi Sati ................................................................... 27

Chapter 6
Tales from the Sacred Sites ....................................................... 35

Chapter 7
The Asura's Threat .................................................................... 38

Chapter 8
The hidden city of Shangri-La .................................................. 43

Chapter 9
Devi Bimala .............................................................................. 47

Chapter 10
The Enigmatic Map ................................................................... 53

Chapter 11
The Lost Path to the Hidden Treasure ...................................... 60

Chapter 12
The star map ............................................................................. 66

Chapter 13
 A letter from the unknown...........................................................73

Chapter 14
 The Amulet's Secret....................................................................76

Chapter 15
 Unveiling the first gem................................................................81

Chapter 16
 Discoveries and Dangers.............................................................85

Chapter 17
 A Slippery Escape ......................................................................88

Chapter 18
 The Hidden World's Calling .......................................................92

Chapter 19
 Chronicles of the Hidden Dawn .................................................97

# Chapter 1

# Prologue: The Awakening

The three companions who will run the risk of life and limb for this quest, the journey begins at Rishikesh as their archaeological adventure is marked by sheer anticipation. Despite the coolness in Meenakshi's hazel eyes, excitement was written all over them as she walks ahead of the rest of her companions. Sidhant, on his part has thick jet-black hair while his amber eye color makes him look more composed than ever although he is secretly envying others. Anjali is here too her dark blonde hair cascading down her Shoulder is indeed a masterpiece and contrasting with mossy-green colored orbs playful energy to the group, her quick wit and free-spirited nature keeps the mood light.

As they delve into their work, Meenakshi's intuition leads them to a remarkable discovery – ancient artifacts buried beneath the earth's surface. With each find, their excitement grows, but when they report their progress to their supervisor, Meenakshi receives all the praise.

'We should inform Mr. Sharma,' suggests Anjali.

Meenakshi nods in agreement and glances at Sidhant, who scoffs, 'I am hell no calling that man!'

*Meenakshi's phone begins to ring*, Anjali asks, 'Who is it?' says Anjali

'it's Mr. Sharma', Meenakshi answers, her voice tinged with sarcasm.

'SPEAK OF THE DEVIL!!!!' screams Sidhant.

'Shh! Sidhant you are way too loud' says Meenakshi.

'So, what's the progress?' demands Mr. Sharma as Meenakshi reluctantly picks up.

'Well sir, we just found the artifacts and were about to call you-'

'I KNEW IT ALREADY! I was right about choosing you as the head of this project WELL DONE' hollered Mr. Sharma while interrupting in between Meenakshi's conversation.

'I was right about you guys well now you can send me the report till this evening then?'

'This evening well yes sir but if you would allot us-' probed Meenakshi.

'Ahh well-well you can take your time then, you guys must be really tired, toddles'

Mr. Sharma abruptly hangs up.

'Thank god, he kept the call,' Meenakshi mutters under her breath.

'Seriously, what about us? Even though we were a part of this project,' Sidhant snaps in a covetous tone.

Meenakshi and Anjali exchanged exasperated glances. 'Come off it!' they chime in unison, but Sidhant merely shrugs.

Sidhant's envy simmers as he watches, unable to conceal his frustration.

'Come off it!' said Meenakshi and Anjali together, but Sidhant merely shrugged.

'He is again touched in the head' said Meenakshi heatedly.

Meanwhile, Sidhant finds himself lost in daydreams of receiving all the praise. Unable to control his jealousy, he stomps off, leaving his frustration simmering in his wake.

As the sun starts going down behind the faraway mountains and turns everything into gold, Meenakshi, Sidhant, and Anjali pick up their stuff reluctantly from the excavation site to say goodbye. They are tired but excited at the same time they have made some discoveries today.

Following winding streets of Rishikesh back, they can hear only their footsteps echoing in the distance of the noisy city.

The girl is ahead with her mind full of things they found and Mr. Sharma's deadline; he is behind with his still streamed by irritation at something; she tries to cheer them all up with jokes or laugh – but it doesn't work.

Seeing their hotel in front of them makes them feel relieved. This huge building with its shining lights has never looked so good before – now they know that there's no longer a way to go. They enter wearily, ready to collapse anywhere and sleep for ages.

In their suite, sitting around the table with cups steaming chai on it, they share stories about what happened today. She writes something down already –they need to make a report by evening.

# Chapter 2

# Dreamer's Vision

As Meenakshi's consciousness drifted into the realm of dreams, she found herself standing in the presence of a divine entity beyond comprehension. Vishwamitra, the all-seeing god, towered before her, his form resplendent and awe-inspiring. Eyes, faces, arms, and feet adorned every side of his magnificent being, with wings stretching outward like celestial guardians.

His presence exuded an aura of power and wisdom that transcended mortal understanding. In front of Vishvakarma stood the luminous figure of the nine-armed goddess Shakti holding all the Astra's, radiant in her beauty and grace.

Draped in a resplendent red saree and seated atop a majestic lion, she emanated an aura of divine authority and maternal warmth. Each of her arms bore symbols of cosmic significance, signifying her boundless power and benevolence.

With a voice that resonated like thunder yet soothed like a gentle breeze, Goddess Durga spoke, her words echoing through the chamber of Meenakshi's mind.

'Vishvakarma, I am allotting you the task to create my temple'. Ensure it is hidden well, beyond the reach of the Asuras. When the time is right, it shall reveal itself to all my devotees." And suddenly a great bright light splashed from the goddess's hands and its intensity was so high that Meenakshi was unable to see anything and covered her eyes; she felt the warmth and power of divine energy coursing through her being.

When the radiance subsided, Meenakshi found herself standing beside a serene lake, its waters were mesmerizing and had the blend of crystal blue and emerald, green.

It was surrounded by the snow-capped mountains that reflected its mirror-like surface which created an ethereal vista.

Drawn to her own reflection, Meenakshi approached the water's edge, marveling at the beauty mirrored back at her. But as she gazed into the depths, a chilling sensation crept over her.

She found something emerging from the depths of Meenakshi's subconscious, the figure of the Asura took shape—a being of darkness and malevolence.

With three heads and dark red skin, with eyes that burned with a fiery intensity, two of his teeth were protruding out like a vampire.

He exuded the aura of terror and malevolence. His form was adorned with golden ornaments, a stark contrast to the darkness that cloaked his being.

He had four arms and in one of his hand, he wielded a sword, its blade gleaming with a malevolent energy that sent shivers down Meenakshi's spine.

As the Asura advanced upon her, time seemed to slow to a crawl, Meenakshi's heart raced, her breath caught in her throat as she faced the looming threat before her.

Her eyes widened with terror, her features contorted in a mixture of shock and disbelief. In that moment, she felt as though her very existence hung in the balance, caught between the forces of light and darkness. With each agonizing moment, Asura drew closer, his sword poised to strike. Meenakshi's mind raced with fear and uncertainty, her senses were overwhelmed by the sheer magnitude of the encounter.

In the depths of her soul, she prayed for deliverance, a glimmer of hope amidst the encroaching darkness. And then, just as the blade descended towards her, a blinding light erupted from the depths of her subconscious, engulfing her in its radiant embrace.

In that moment of divine intervention, Meenakshi felt a surge of energy coursing through her being, banishing the darkness and dispelling the terror that had gripped her heart.

With a gasp, Meenakshi awoke from her dream, her body drenched in fear and her mind reeling from the intensity of her vision.

Trembling, she switched off the alarm and gathered her wits, steeling herself for the day ahead.

She headed towards the café where she found Anjali and Sidhant waiting for her and as usual Sidhant was taunting Meenakshi.

'So, what's with that face Meenakshi, suit yourself you look like a- um never mind," said Sidhant.

'I look like A WOT!' yelled Meenakshi 'A SLOTH, you know, just by seeing that face of yours ruins my entire mood' Sidhant retorted with a smirk.

'You better keep your wits about you' leered Meenakshi.

'Keep you cool guys you guys always fights like cats and dogs' snapped Anjali Trying to diffuse the tension, Anjali added,

'Come on, let's not ruin our breakfast with this nonsense. Meenakshi, maybe Sidhant is just jealous that he can't pull off a sloth-like look as effortlessly as you.'

Meenakshi couldn't help but crack a smile at Anjali's attempt to lighten the mood.

'Well, if looking like a sloth means I get to laze around all day, maybe I should take it as a compliment,' she quipped, her irritation melting away.

Sidhant rolled his eyes playfully. 'Please, Meenakshi, spare us all from witnessing your attempt at sloth impersonation,' he teased, earning a chuckle from Anjali.

Meenakshi shot back, 'Oh, don't worry, Sidhant. I wouldn't want to steal the spotlight from your award-winning impersonation of a GRUMPY OLD MAN.' Sidhant feigned offense, placing a hand dramatically over his heart.

'I'll have you know that my grumpy old man impression is a crowd favorite,' he declared, earning a round of laughter from the nearby tables.

Anjali noticed the change in Meenakshi's demeanor and furrowed her brow in concern.

'Hey, Meenakshi, you seem a bit off. Is everything okay? Meenakshi snapped out of her reverie, her expression clouded with uncertainty.

'I had this really weird dream last night,' she began, her voice trailing off as she struggled to find the right words.

Before she could continue, Sidhant let out a snort of laughter, earning a glare from Meenakshi. Ignoring his interruption, she forged ahead, recounting the surreal encounter with Vishwamitra, Goddess Shakti, and the ominous figure of the Asura. Sidhant scoffed dismissively.

'Come on, Meenakshi, it was just a nightmare. Dreams don't mean anything. You're reading too much into it.' Anjali shook her head, her expression thoughtful.

'Actually, Sidhant, there's a lot of evidence to suggest that dreams do have meaning. They can be reflections of our subconscious thoughts and emotions.' Sidhant rolled his eyes, unconvinced.

'Please, Anjali, spare us the psychoanalysis. It's just a dream.' Anjali shot him a pointed look, her tone firm.

'Dreams can be powerful messages from our inner selves. Meenakshi's dream Sounded significant, especially considering its mystical elements.'

Meenakshi nodded in agreement, grateful for Anjali's support.

'Exactly it felt so real, like there was a deeper meaning behind it.'

Anjali turned to Meenakshi; her gaze was curious.

'What did the mystical beings in your dream look like? Can you describe them in detail?' Before Meenakshi could respond, Sidhant interjected, his tone dripping with skepticism.

'Seriously? You're indulging in this nonsense too, Anjali? You guys are just being delusional.' Anjali's patience wore thin, her voice sharp.

'Shut up, Sidhant. You know nothing about the power of dreams Meenakshi DO NOT LISTEN TO THAT IGNORANT'

'The Vishwamitra, the all-seeing god, was magnificent and awe-inspiring,' she began, her voice steady despite the memories flooding back.

'He had eyes, faces, arms, and feet on every side, with wings stretching outward like celestial guardians. His presence exuded power and wisdom beyond mortal comprehension.'

Pausing for a moment to collect her thoughts, Meenakshi continued, 'Goddess Shakti, on the other hand, was radiant and ethereal. Draped in a resplendent red saree and seated atop a majestic lion." Meenakshi's voice faltered slightly as she recalled the figure of the Asura, his dark presence casting a shadow over her memories.

'The Asura was… terrifying,' she admitted, her tone somber 'It had three heads, dark crimson skin, and eyes that burned with a fiery intensity, he exuded an aura of malevolence and darkness. His form was adorned with golden ornaments, a stark contrast to the darkness that cloaked his being.' Anjali listened intently, her eyes wide with curiosity. 'Wow, that sounds intense,' she remarked, her voice filled with awe. Before Meenakshi could respond, Sidhant scoffed dismissively.

'Oh, please. It's just a bunch of nonsense. You're letting your imagination run wild, Meenakshi.'

Meenakshi shot him a withering glare, her frustration mounting. 'This wasn't just my imagination, Sidhant. It felt too real to be dismissed so easily.'

Anjali placed a comforting hand on Meenakshi's arm, her gaze unwavering. 'I believe you, Meenakshi. Dreams can be powerful messages from our subconscious. There's more to this than meets the eye.'

Meenakshi felt a surge of gratitude towards Anjali for her unwavering support.

After which they continue to have their breakfast and after it's over Meenakshi and her team prepare to send off the report and take their promised leave, they gather for a final discussion before parting ways.

Meenakshi, leaning against a nearby table, flips through the pages of the report one last we'd uncovered so much in such a short time.

Sidhant, the pragmatist, crosses his arms and nods in agreement.

'Yeah, well, let's hope Mr. Sharma sees it the same way. We don't want him breathing down our necks for any missed details.'

Meenakshi rolls her eyes, chuckling softly 'Always the optimist, Sidhant.' Anjali interjects, her tone teasing.

'Oh, come on, Sidhant. Let's give Meenakshi some credit for once. She's been leading the charge this whole time, and I think we've done a thorough job.'

Sidhant raises an eyebrow, a smirk playing at the corners of his lips. 'Well, I suppose I can give credit were credit's due. Just don't let it go to your head, Meenakshi.'

Meenakshi mock-scowls at Sidhant before her expression softens into a smile.

'Thanks, guys I Couldn't have done it without you both.'

With the report finalized and their leave approved, the team takes a moment to savor their accomplishments and reflect on the journey they've shared together.

'I think this covers everything we found,' she remarks, glancing up at her teammates.

'It's been quite a journey, hasn't it?' Anjali nods, a wistful smile tugging at her lips 'Definitely I would've never imagined things would end so soon'

'You know, we've traveled so far and had the privilege of being in such a holy place,' Meenakshi begins, her voice infused with reverence.

'It would be a shame to leave without experiencing the Ganga Aarti." Anjali's face lights up with agreement. 'That sounds like a wonderful idea, Meenakshi! We've been so caught up with work that we haven't had a chance to truly immerse ourselves in the spiritual atmosphere of Rishikesh.

'Sidhant nods in approval, a rare smile gracing his features. 'I'm in,' he declares, surprising his teammates with his enthusiasm.

'It'll be a nice change of pace from digging up artifacts all day.'

# Chapter 3

# A Night of Revelation

As the flames of the Ganga Aarti cast their golden glow upon the sacred waters of the Ganges, Meenakshi, Anjali, and Sidhant stand in silent awe, their hearts stirred by the mystical beauty of the ancient ritual.

The rhythmic chants of the priest's echo in their ears, mingling with the gentle lapping of the river and creating an atmosphere of divine reverence and spiritual awakening.

In the flickering light of the oil lamps, Meenakshi's frosty eyes gleam with a newfound intensity, her gaze drawn to the Ethereal dance of shadows on the water's surface. Beside her, Sidhant's raven-black hair seems to catch fire in the golden light, his amber eyes reflecting the flickering flames with a mix of wonder and skepticism.

And Anjali, with her mossy eyes shining with an inner light, seems to be enveloped in a halo of divine grace, her presence a beacon of warmth and comfort amidst the solemnity of the ritual.

As the Ganga Aarti reaches its crescendo, Meenakshi feels a pull towards the river's edge, drawn by an unseen force that whispers of ancient mysteries waiting to be unveiled.

With each step closer to the water, she feels a sense of anticipation building within her, her heart pounding with the promise of revelation. Leaning over the edge of the river, Meenakshi peers into the dark depths below, her reflection shimmering on the surface like a ghostly apparition.

But as she gazes into the rippling waters, she sees something else—a figure emerging from the depths, bathed in celestial light and radiating an aura of divine grace.

Meenakshi's breath catches in her throat as she beholds the figure before her, her eyes widening in disbelief and wonder. It is Goddess Shakti herself, the embodiment of divine femininity and cosmic power.

In that moment of divine revelation, Meenakshi feels a surge of energy coursing through her veins, her spirit lifting with the

knowledge that she stands in the presence of the divine. Slowly, The reflection of Goddess Shakti vanishes within the water, leaving Meenakshi in a state of awe and wonder.

As the sound of the Aarti and the ringing of bells fill the air, Meenakshi and Sidhant are both overwhelmed by a sudden sense of divinity.

They are reluctant to leave the sacred space, their hearts filled with reverence and awe for the ancient rituals and timeless traditions unfolding before them.

Together, Meenakshi, Anjali, and Sidhant stand at the water's edge; their souls alight with the divine presence of the place. In that timeless moment, they are united in purpose and faith; their hearts open to the mysteries of the universe and the wonders that lie beyond. After the Ganga Aarti ends, Meenakshi, Anjali, and Sidhant find themselves deeply moved by the experience.

They share a moment of silence, each lost in their own thoughts.

'That was... incredible,' Meenakshi finally says, her voice soft with awe. Anjali nods, her eyes shining.

'I've never felt such peace and reverence before. It was like being in another world.'

Sidhant, usually the pragmatic one, simply nods, a rare sense of wonder on his face

Reluctantly, they start back to the hotel Meenakshi returns to her room after the Ganga Aarti, still feeling the lingering effects of the divine atmosphere. As she scrolls through social media, she notices that Sidhant is still active online.

Concerned, she gives him a call, reminding him of their early flight the next morning.

Sidhant admits that he's finding it hard to sleep, still caught up in the aura of the Ganga Aarti.

Meenakshi agrees, sharing her own sense of the profound experience they had just witnessed.

But Sidhant quickly shifts the conversation, stating that it's late and he needs to sleep. Meenakshi agrees, though she's left with a strange feeling lingering in her mind. As she drifts off to sleep, she finds herself transported back to the banks of the Ganges, the scene of the Ganga Aarti still vivid in her mind. The river flows gently beside her, its waters reflecting the flickering light of the oil lamps.

There's an otherworldly calmness in the air, a sense of reverence that permeates every corner of her consciousness.

As Meenakshi stands by the river, she notices that she's alone, the usual hustle and bustle of the Aarti is absent. Yet, there's a strange tranquility in the solitude, as if she's been granted a private audience with the divine.

Suddenly, the sound of anklets draws her attention, and she turns to see a figure approaching from the shadows. The figure is bathed in a radiant glow, her form obscured by the brilliance of her aura. Meenakshi can make out the outline of a woman, her features softened by the ethereal light that surrounds her.

The woman's presence is overwhelming; her energy pulsating with a divine power that Meenakshi can feel deep in her soul. She holds a Trishul in one hand and wears a crescent moon in her hair, symbols of her celestial authority.

As the woman draws nearer, Meenakshi is filled with a sense of awe and reverence.

It's as if she's in the presence of a deity, a being of boundless wisdom and grace.

The woman speaks her voice feels like music to Meenakshi's ears. She urges Meenakshi not to leave, her words carrying a weight of urgency and importance.

Meenakshi can feel the truth of the woman's words resonating within her, a deep knowing that transcends logic and reason. But before Meenakshi can respond, a blinding light engulfs her, forcing her to shield her eyes.

When the light fades, she finds herself back in her room, the memory of the woman's presence still lingering in her mind like a fading dream.

As Meenakshi wakes from her dream, she's left with a profound sense of wonder and curiosity. Who was the luminous figure she encountered by the river? What message was she trying to convey? Meenakshi knows that she may never have the answers, but the memory of her dream will stay with her forever.

The next morning, Meenakshi shares her strange dream with Sidhant and Anjali, feeling reluctant to leave Rishikesh.

Sidhant dismisses her concerns by telling her that she is over thinking.

Meenakshi reluctantly agrees, but the feeling of unease still remains to linger around her.

As they head out of the hotel towards the airport, the weather starts to change, but they pay little heed.

However, as they reach the airport, they find themselves caught in a fierce storm, causing their taxi to get stranded. By the time they reach the airport, they've missed their flight due to the adverse weather conditions.

Meenakshi can't shake the feeling that her dream was a warning, a message from the divine urging them to stay. As Anjali suggests taking the train instead, Meenakshi and Sidhant quickly agree, eager to find an alternative mode of transportation.

They leave the airport and make their way to the train station, hopeful that they'll soon be on their way home. However, as theyarrive at the station, their hopes are dashed by an announcement echoing through the crowded terminal.

The voice on the loudspeaker informs them that all trains have been cancelled due to the heavy rainfall and storm. Meenakshi, Sidhant, and Anjali exchange dismayed looks, realizing that their journey home has been thwarted once again. They're left stranded in the bustling station, unsure of what to do next as the storm rages on outside. Unable to think, what to do next Anjali comes up with an way.

'Meenakshi's dream did made sense' asserted Anjali

'How come' probed Sidhant

'Well, Meenakshi had the dream about the goddess where she was told to not leave the place plus don't you think that it is extremely oddly that all of us are feeling reluctant to leave this place?' says Anjali.

'I don't buy it please use your noodles for god's sake' nagged Sidhant.

'KEEP YOUR WITS ABOUT YOU' snapped Meenakshi.

'Exactly I have a great plan let us visit a saint and tell them our problems I know someone here; we can go meet them' insisted Anjali.

'I'm so psyched that's a really great opinion' says Meenakshi

# Chapter 4

# Vishwakarma's Legacy

As they reach the ashram, its swastika-shaped architecture leaves them in awe. The ashram's intricate design, lush gardens, and serene atmosphere are breathtaking.

Anjali, captivated by the beauty of the place, suddenly exclaims, "Wow, look at this place! I've heard about this holy ashram, but I never imagined it would be this beautiful."

Meenakshi and Sidhant nod in agreement, equally mesmerized by the serene surroundings. The ashram is adorned with vibrant he flowers, and the air is filled with the soothing sound of bird

'I think we should go in now,' Meenakshi says, her voice filled with anticipation.

Just as they are about to enter, Anjali has a sudden moment of panic. 'Oh no, I left my phone in the taxi! I should go and get it.'

Meenakshi tries to reassure her, 'Don't worry, Anjali. Your phone will be safe. The taxi isn't going anywhere until we return.'

'But still, I need it,' Anjali insists, her urgency evident.

'I'll be back in a jiffy. You guys go ahead; I'll catch up soon.'

Sidhant, raising an eyebrow, mutters, 'Why is she behaving so weirdly lately?'

'She said she'll join us soon. Let's just go in,' Meenakshi responds, slightly amused by the situation.

As Anjali rushes off to retrieve her phone, Meenakshi and Sidhant make their way into the ashram. The entrance leads them into a large courtyard, surrounded by beautifully carved pillars and statues. The peaceful ambiance immediately puts them at ease, yet They feel slightly disoriented by the multiple pathways leading in different directions.

'Which way should we go?' Sidhant wonders aloud, looking around in confusion.

Before they can decide, a child dressed in a beautiful green sari with long hair and a few ornaments approaches them. Her forehead is adorned with a red bindi, and her skin glows with the yellow Chandan smeared across it. The child exudes an air of calm and purity.

'Whom do you want to meet?' the child asks, her voice sweet and gentle.

Meenakshi steps forward and explains, 'We've heard that a saint lives here. We've come to meet him.'

The child nods, understandingly. 'Oh, I see. You want to meet my father. I'll take you to him.'

Guided by the child, they walk through the ashram's serene pathways, passing by devotees and monks engaged in meditation and prayer.

The tranquility of the place is overwhelming, and they can't help but feel a deep sense of peace.

As they approach a large, beautifully decorated house within the ashram, they notice a huge idol of Goddess Shakti inside, surrounded by offerings and flowers. The sight is both awe-inspiring and humbling.

Sidhant, curious about their young guide, asks, 'By the way, what's your name?'

The child smiles and replies, 'My name is Tripura.'

'Tripura! That's such a pretty name,' Sidhant compliments, earning a shy smile from the child.

Tripura then points to a saint dressed in a pure white garment with a red border, with Kumkum applied to his forehead.

'There, that's my father,' she says.

As Meenakshi turns back to thank Sharda, she sees the child running away, disappearing into the ashram's labyrinthine pathways. She smiles, feeling a sense of wonder at the encounter.

Approaching the saint, they bow respectfully. The saint looks up from his meditation and greets them warmly.

'What brings you here at this hour, my children? Haven't you seen the board outside those states during this time, outsiders are not allowed to visit?'

Meenakshi immediately apologizes, 'We didn't see the board. We're very sorry for the intrusion.'

The saint waves off their apology with a gentle smile. "It's fine, but next time, please check the time before entering."

'Sure, we'll be more mindful next time,' Meenakshi assures him.

The saint studies them for a moment before asking, "By the way, I haven't seen you here before. Is this your first time here?"

Sidhant and Meenakshi nodded in agreement.

The saint then asks, 'How did you find your way to me? Most people tend to wander around.'

Meenakshi explains, 'Your daughter brought us here. She took us through the ashram and pointed towards you, saying, 'That is my father,' and that's how we ended up here.'

The saint's expression changes to one of disbelief.

'My daughter? That's not possible. I have no children.'

Sidhant interjects, 'Then who was the girl that brought us here?'

Intrigued, the saint asks, 'What did she look like?'

Meenakshi describes Tripura's appearance in detail: 'She was a young girl, dressed in a beautiful green sari with long hair and a few ornaments. She had a red bindi on her forehead and yellow Chandan smeared across it.'

The saint's eyes widen in astonishment. He leads them to a temple inside the house, where they see an idol of Goddess Shakti dressed exactly as Meenakshi described Sharda.

Puzzled, the saint admits, 'I haven't opened the curtains since morning. How did she describe the idol so accurately?'

A sense of understanding dawns on the saint as he realizes the divine intervention at play. Smiling warmly, he says, 'You are surely fortunate. Ask me anything you want to know.'

Meenakshi then begins to narrate her entire dream, eager to seek answers from the wise saint. As she speaks, the saint listens intently, nodding occasionally. When she finishes, he takes a deep breath and begins to share a story:

'The story of Vishwakarma sounds very familiar to me. Let me narrate the complete story. This is not recorded anywhere, but it has been passed down through generations.

After the Samudra Manthan, when the devas gained their power by consuming Amrit, the asuras' power began to decline. The asuras turned to their guru, Shukracharya, for guidance. Concerned for the asuras, Shukracharya suggested that there was one way: Goddess Shakti's hidden temple, constructed by Vishwakarma, is located on Bhulok, the earth.

The key to the temple is a gem, which was broken into four pieces and hidden to keep it away from the asuras.

'But why are the asuras after the temple?' Meenakshi asks.

The saint replies, 'Legends believe that a part of the Amrit is hidden there. Some say there's a portal to immense wealth and prosperity, while others suggest a weapon more powerful than Indra's astra is concealed within. No one knows for sure, as the temple gates have never been opened.'

The narration leaves Sidhant and Meenakshi thunderstruck. Meenakshi asks, 'Do you have any manuscripts or something that talks about it?'

The saint nods and says, 'I might have something.' After a while, he brings out an extremely old manuscript. 'This is where it is mentioned,' he says, handing it to them.

As they carefully examine the ancient manuscript, the weight of their discovery sinks in, and they realize they are on the brink of an extraordinary adventure.

## Chapter 5

# Echoes of Devi Sati

After taking the manuscript with them and thanking the saint, Meenakshi and Sidhant step out of the temple. As they exit, they see Anjali rushing towards them, her face flushed with urgency.

'Sorry, sorry, I'm so late!' Anjali pants, looking genuinely apologetic.

Sidhant, raising an eyebrow, asks, 'Where have you been? Does it take that long to get your phone?'

Anjali explains, 'I got a call from my mother. I got so caught up talking with her that I forgot I needed to rush back to the ashram. I'm really sorry, guys.'

Meenakshi, offering a reassuring smile, says, 'It's fine, Anjali. We'll tell you everything that happened inside once we get back to the hotel. I don't think it's appropriate to discuss these things here.'

With that, they make their way back to the hotel. Once settled in Meenakshi's room, they gather around a small table, the ancient manuscript laid out before them. Meenakshi begins recounting their encounter with the saint and the mysterious child, Sharda.

Anjali listens, wide-eyed, as Meenakshi describes the entire sequence of events. When Meenakshi finishes, Anjali is thunderstruck.

'Wow, this is incredible,' Anjali breathes, staring at the manuscript in awe.

They start analyzing the manuscript together. Each page of the manuscript is beautifully illustrated, with intricate art styles that capture their attention. The text is written in elegant Sanskrit script, which only adds to its allure.

Sidhant, frowning slightly, says, "It's in Sanskrit. My Sanskrit isn't great."

Anjali smirks and says, "Have you forgotten that I am a Sanskrit scholar? Let me take a look."

Anjali begins to read each page carefully, translating the ancient text for them. As she turns to the last page, her expression changes to one of excitement.

"Everything written in the previous pages is exactly what the priest told you about. But listen to this, this page is important," Anjali says, her voice tinged with anticipation.

She then recites a shloka from the manuscript:

'रत्नस्य चरणो भिन्नम्,

चतुर्भिः खण्डैः गुप्तम्।

यत्र मिलन्ति भवति, व

िश्वकर्मणस्य दर्शनम्॥'

'The gem is broken into four pieces, hidden away in four places. Where they come together, the vision of Vishwakarma appears.'

Anjali continues, 'The last page describes the gem. It talks about how the gem was split into four parts and hidden in different locations to protect its power.'

Meenakshi, intrigued, asks, 'Does it say anything about where these pieces are hidden?'

Anjali scans the text, her finger tracing the elegant Sanskrit script. 'It doesn't specify exact locations but mentions clues about their whereabouts. It seems these clues are embedded within the art on each page.'

Sidhant, now fully engaged, says, 'So we need to decode the art and the text together to find the pieces of the gem.'

Meenakshi nods, 'Exactly. We need to piece together these clues to uncover the hidden locations.'

They start reading the manuscript, examining the illustrations and text meticulously. Each page presents a new riddle, a new clue to decipher.

Their excitement builds as they realize they are on the verge of a significant discovery.

The load of their job hits them in the night as they toil away. In their narrative, they are not merely revealing an old work of art; they are subjected to a trail which has been devised by the deities, with their lives interwoven through this adventure

As they turned the page, they saw an image of Lord Shiva in his fierce Bhairav form, holding Goddess Sati in his arms. In front of them stood Lord Vishnu, wielding the Sudarshan Chakra. Below the image, a Shlok was written:

"शिवस्य बाहुभ्याम् धारिता,

सती देवी दिव्या।

विष्णुं चक्रेण रक्षन्तम्,

रत्नांशोः सुरक्षितम्॥"

Meenakshi, Sidhant, and Anjali were mesmerized by the vivid imagery and the profound meaning behind the words.

The shloka conveyed that the *remnants of the sacred gems were kept safely under the watchful eyes of the divine Goddess Sati*, protected by the power of Lord Vishnu and the strength of Lord Shiva.

Sidhant scratched his head and said, 'Goddess Sati, I have heard this name before, but I can't seem to recall the details.'

Meenakshi and Anjali exchanged incredulous looks and exclaimed in unison, 'Seriously, Sidhant, how could you be so dumb?'

'Guys, stop overreacting,' Sidhant retorted with a smirk., and don't forget my qualifications before calling me dumb."

Meenakshi sighed and said, 'Let me narrate you the story.'

'Sati, also known as Dakshayani (daughter of Daksha), is the Hindu goddess of marital felicity and longevity. She is worshipped as an aspect of the mother goddess Shakti. Sati was the first wife of Shiva; the other being Parvati, who was Sati's reincarnation After her death. Devi Sati is Adi Shakti herself. Daksha, blinded by his ego hated Lord Shiva, even though he is one of the Tridev.

Daksha once invited all deities to a great yajna, except for his daughter Sati and Shiva. Sati decided to attend the ceremony and was discredited by her father. Unable to control herself from rage over both what her father had said about Sati's husband being vulgar as well as this insult against her own dignity, the goddess took on Adi Shakti's form and set herself ablaze in the fire.

'As for Shiva, he was overwhelmed with grief carrying her corpse all around the globe recalling their happy moments together when Vishnu cut off pieces of Sati's body using the Sudarshana Chakra so that she could be reincarnated; those pieces landed on earth becoming sacred places called Shakti Peethas. She lives there to become Shakti herself at those sites which become very sacred ones in their worshipping rituals where devotees make sites of goddess' love and thus, they have been connecting her energy since ancient times.'

Sidhant listened intently, nodding slowly. 'I see, that's quite a powerful story. Thanks for the refresher, Meenakshi. It all makes sense now.

Anjali added, 'It's not just a story, Sidhant. It's the essence of divine energy and the connection we're experiencing here. This manuscript and everything happening to us might be part of something much bigger.'

Meenakshi agreed, 'Exactly, Anjali. This place, these experiences, they're all interconnected. We need to be careful and respectful as we uncover more about this mystery.'

Sidhant shook his head and said, 'But there is 51 Shakti Peethas spread all over the world. We can't possibly visit each other, can we?'

Meenakshi pondered for a moment. 'There must be another way. We need to narrow it down further.'

Anjali, deep in thought, said, 'Let's think about the clues we have. The manuscript mentioned 'the remains of the gems are kept safely under the eyes of the divine goddess Sati.' We need to interpret this clue carefully.'

Sidhant added, 'We need to find a connection to the specific Shakti Peetha that fits this description. Maybe something related to the divine goddess Sati herself.'

Meenakshi suddenly remembered something. 'What if we look for a Shakti Peetha that is directly connected to an important aspect of the goddess Sati? There must be historical or mythological texts that can give us more information.'

Anjali nodded. 'We should research the specific Shakti Peethas and their unique significance. There's bound to be some literature or references that can guide us to the right one.'

Sidhant sighed but looked more hopeful.

'It's still a long shot, but it's better than visiting all 51. Let's focus on the ones that have unique attributes or significant myths related to goddess Sati.'

Meenakshi agreed. 'We should start with the most well-known ones and see if there are any legends or stories that match our clues. It will take some research, but we're on the right track.'

Anjali smiled. 'I have a few contacts who specialize in ancient texts and mythology. They might be able to help us narrow it down.'

Sidhant added, 'And we can also investigate any historical records or local folklore. Sometimes, the locals have stories passed down through generations that aren't recorded in official texts.'

With a newfound sense of purpose, they resolved to distribute the responsibilities among themselves. Meenakshi and Anjali intended to approach their contacts and carry out research on Shakti Peethas while Sidhant would investigate local myths and ancient documents.

No one was under any illusion about how difficult the trek ahead would be, but faith in the Divine helped them stay strong enough.

This was the jewel that lied out there beneath the gaze of Sati, the goddess herself; and they were very much committed to finding it.

# Chapter 6

# Tales from the Sacred Sites

Sidhant, Meenakshi, and Anjali were deeply engrossed in their research. They split up for the day to gather more information. Sidhant decided to visit the local library and speak with locals, while Meenakshi and Anjali focused on reading ancient scriptures.

Later that evening, they reconvened in the library to share their findings.

'Alright, what did you find out today, Sidhant?' Anjali asked, curiosity evident in her voice.

Sidhant leaned forward, eager to reveal his findings. He said, 'There are some very interesting myths I stumbled upon. For one, there's Assam's Kamakhya Temple. Legend has it that goddess Sati's womb and veloce fell there. The temple has become known for its profound mystique and tantric use. Locals speak of secret rooms within the temple complex as well as magical items that have been left behind by its founders. This could be a major clue.'

Meenakshi's eyes widened with interest. 'Kamakhya Temple... I've heard it's a place of immense spiritual power.'

That's not all," Sidhant continued. 'I also found tales about the Jwala Mukhi Temple in Himachal Pradesh, where goddess Sati's tongue is believed to have fallen. This temple is unique because it doesn't have an idol but a constantly burning blue flame. Local folklore speaks of hidden treasures and divine blessings there.'

Anjali nodded, taking notes. 'These places are definitely worth investigating. What else?'

Sidhant leaned back, thinking. 'There's also the story of VindhyaVasini Temple, where goddess Sati's heart is said to have fallen. According to local legends, this temple is a place of immense power and divine presence. Myths surrounding the temple often include references to hidden divine artifacts.'

Sidhant looked thoughtful. 'But there is 51 Shakti Peethas spread all over the world. We can't visit each place, can we?'

Meenakshi shook her head. 'There must be another way. We need to find more clues to narrow it down.

Meenakshi then spoke up. 'Anjali and I also did some digging. Out of all the 51 Shakti Peethas, we identified four prominent ones: Tara Tarini near Berhampur, Bimala inside the Jagannath Temple in Puri, Kamakhya near Guwahati, and Dakshina Kalika in Kolkata.'

Anjali added, 'And remember, the pieces of the gem are four. The prominent Peethas are also four. It feels like we're heading in the right direction.'

Anjali, determined, said, 'We'll keep researching. The answers are out there. We just need to connect the dots.'

The group persevered in their analysis, with each member even more resolute than before to decode the enigmas surrounding Shakti Peethas and undiscovered treasures.

# Chapter 7

# The Asura's Threat

Late night saw three people come together in a library for their discoveries' discussion. Tension permeated through as if drops of liquid nitrogen were injected into them. Out of nowhere, Meenakshi saw flickering shadows from the corner of her eye while calming whispers coming from pages.

'Do you feel that?' she asked, her voice barely above a whisper.

Anjali looked up from an ancient manuscript. 'Feel what?'

'Like we're being watched,' Meenakshi replied, her eyes darting around the dimly lit room.

Sidhant shrugged, trying to appear nonchalant.

'It's just your imagination, Meenakshi. We're the only ones here.' However, when it was twelfth hour, everything had become worse. A chilling wind swept across the library, blowing out most of the candles. There were violent shadows that slithered up and down the white wall of the room like snakes along a branch and all voices sounded louder. Anjali was still holding the book so tightly. "There's something amiss.'

Before they could even realize what was going on, some off black shadows appeared at the corners of the room. They were moving shapes with no fixed position only their colors changing resembling smoke. Evil filled the space all around them making it hard to breathe normally.

'Who are you?' Sidhant demanded, trying to keep his voice steady.

The shadows coalesced into more defined shapes, revealing humanoid forms with glowing red eyes. One of them stepped forward, its voice a hiss.

'We are the Asuras, and you are meddling in affairs beyond your comprehension.' Meenakshi's heart pounded. 'What do you want?'

'The gems,' Asura hissed. 'They belong to us.'

An attack suddenly came from the Asuras. Sidhant, Meenakshi, and Anjali were conceiving methods of shielding themselves. Meenakshi remembered a protective chant from their research and started reciting a powerful mantra when their shield was created by air around them that glittered bright suggesting it has some kind of magic for a brief moment before dispersing away into nothingness. 'We can't hold them off for long!' yelled Meenakshi.

Sidhant within reached out for an old scroll with another invocation he started saying aloud; it started shining whereby the Asuras got pushed back farther. Illuminated in the middle of the room was a circle formed out of light like it was out of fiction books that we have read so many times before. From this bending cloud streaming radar inside emerged a figure donning robe inscribed with these inscriptions which represented ages long past a they held onto his or her scepter.

'Stand back, children!' the guardian commanded.

Sidhant, still shaken, couldn't resist a quip. 'Did you just walk out of a fantasy novel?'

The guardian's gaze remained stern. 'I am here to protect you from a very real threat.'

Strike the earth with your staff and it will send light waves across the room. The Asuras let out a wail then evaporated into thin air, returning back into shadows.

The guardian looked at them three with a serious expression. 'What you have just seen is the real risk of your journey. The Asuras are merciless; they will do anything just to get their hands on those stones.' Meenakshi appended sarcastically, "Anyhow we know we aren't tripping." In response, the guardian gave them a tiny well-carved amulet "That is for some preservation. Always carry it as your companion"

Meenakshi accepted the amulet, her resolve hardening. 'We won't let the Asuras win. We'll find the gems and protect them.'

The guardian nodded. 'You must. For the fate of the world depends on it.'

As the portal's shimmering glow began to fade, Sidhant squinted at it suspiciously.

'Okay, seriously, did we just stumble out of a Marvel movie? Because I'm pretty sure I saw Doctor Strange sipping tea over there.'

Anjali chuckled, shaking her head.

'If only we had a superhero to guide us through this mess.'

Meenakshi shot them a wry smile.

'Well, we do have each other, and that's close enough, right?'

Sidhant raised an eyebrow. 'I'm not so sure. Anjali's powers might rival Thor's hammer, but I'm not convinced you can summon the Hulk with your meditation chants, Meenakshi.'

Anjali rolled her eyes. 'You've been watching too many superhero movies, Sidhant.'

'Just trying to make sense of this craziness, 'Sidhant retorted with a grin.

Meanwhile, Meenakshi pocketed the ancient paper with a determined gleam in her eye.

'Who needs superheroes when you have us? Now, let's go find the parts of the gem and maybe recruit our own Avengers while we're at it.'

With a mix of laughter and determination, they turned away from the now-closed portal, ready to embark on their next adventure.

# Chapter 8

# The hidden city of Shangri-La

Late into the night, the library became a haven of hushed excitement and whispered theories. The trio gathered around a large wooden table, the soft glow of a nearby lamp casting long shadows on the walls filled with ancient books. Suddenly, the shimmering circular portal reappeared, and the saints stepped through it.

'You are the chosen ones,' the lead saint announced. 'You cannot step back. This is a diminishing future as it is impossible for anyone to tell exactly what the Asuras are plotting hence why you should move faster and gather all of the gem's pieces before they can be found by them. Begin searching from Jagannath Puri because we'll meet elsewhere once you find its first part. For now, hold on these amulets since they may offer some protection, but only up to a certain extent." The saints handed them protective amulets and continued, 'We shall meet again after you find the first gem.' Then they entered their way through the portal. In its closing moments a vintage brown paper fell down; on it was inscribed "Shangri-La".

Anjali's eyes widened in recognition. Shangri-La….. The legendary hidden city.'

Sidhant's skepticism momentarily wavered.

'Are you telling me we're going to find a mythical city now?'

Meenakshi tucked the paper into her pocket, her determination unwavering.

'We've already encountered Asuras and divine guardians. Why not add a hidden city to the mix?' With a shared glance, they stepped away from the closing portal, their resolve steeled. 'We'll meet again,' Meenakshi called out into the dissipating light, her voice carrying the weight of destiny. 'When the time is right.'

As the realization settled in, Sidhant turned to the group, puzzled. 'Can anyone here tell me what exactly Shangri-La is?'

Anjali took a deep breath, ready to share her knowledge.

'Shambhala is a mythical city said to be in the Himalayas. It is also known as 'Shangri-La' and 'Aghartha'.

The word 'Shangri-La' is Sanskrit for 'place of peace' or 'land of happiness'. In Tibetan Buddhist tradition, Shangri-La is a spiritual kingdom where all citizens have achieved enlightenment and live in a paradise free of evil.

It is a place of pure knowledge, harmony, and well-being, where people live in harmony and some even live to be over 100 years old. According to legend, Shangri-La is only accessible to those with pure hearts and is hidden deep underground in the mountainous regions of Eurasia, possibly in the Himalayas of Tibet. It is also mentioned in the Kalachakra Tantra, and the Bon scriptures refer to a related land called Tagzig Olmo Lung Ring.'

She continued, 'In Altai folklore, Mount Belukha is believed to be the gateway to Shangri-La. Modern Buddhist scholars seem to conclude that Shangri-La is in the higher reaches of the Himalayas, in what is now called the Dhaula Dhar Mountains around McLeod Ganj.

Shangri-La is also known as Gyan Ganj. Gyan Ganj is a mythical and legendary place, often referred to as a fabled hidden city or kingdom in the Himalayas.

It is part of various Indian and Tibetan folklore and is sometimes associated with the concept of Shangri-La in Tibetan Buddhism. According to the myths, Gyan Ganj is a land of highly enlightened beings or sages who possess extraordinary knowledge and powers. It is believed that these beings are immortal and exist in a state of eternal bliss, living in seclusion from the outside world.'

After Anjali's detailed explanation, both Meenakshi and Sidhant looked at her in astonishment.

Meenakshi couldn't help but ask, 'How on earth do you know so much about this?'

Anjali smiled, slightly embarrassed. 'I love researching such mystical topics. I found this one particularly interesting, so I studied it extensively.

Sidhant chuckled, shaking his head in disbelief. 'Of course you did. Well, at least we have an expert on our team.'

Meenakshi nodded. 'Yes, and with this knowledge, we're one step closer to uncovering the secrets of the hidden temple built by Vishwakarma.'

Anjali added, 'And we need to stay ahead of the Asuras. Our journey is just beginning.'

# Chapter 9

## Devi Bimala

As dawn broke, Meenakshi, Sidhant, and Anjali reconvened at the cafe, their minds were set to move forward towards the next step. Sidhant stirred his coffee, lost in thought.

'Mr. Sharma is going to be a problem,' he said, breaking the silence.

Meenakshi nodded.

'He's too involved in our every move. We need to execute with a plan to keep him occupied.'

Anjali, always the strategist, leaned in. 'We could send him on a wild goose chase. Tell him we need crucial historical data from a remote archive.'

Sidhant smirked.

'You mean, get him to chase a lead that doesn't exist? I like it. But we need it to be convincing.'

Meenakshi added, 'We should mention a reputed historian who could provide exclusive insights, someone Sharma wouldn't dare to ignore.'

Anjali's eyes lit up instantly.

'How about Professor Dhruv from the University of Madras? He's well-known and reclusive, he will be a perfect distraction.'

They quickly drafted an email to Mr. Sharma, detailing the supposed importance of meeting Professor Dhruv and obtaining specific documents related to the Jagannath Temple's history. They emphasized it how this information was critical to their research and had potential breakthrough.

After sending the email, they waited, nervously sipping their drinks. An hour later, Mr. Sharma replied with enthusiasm, confirming he would head to Chennai immediately.

Sidhant fist-pumped the air. 'One problem down. Now, let's focus on Jagannath Puri.'

The next morning, they all met at the cafe for breakfast, their resolve was firmer than ever.

Sidhant broke the silence, 'We need to head to Jagannath Puri as soon as possible. The saints said it's where we'll find the first piece of the gem.'

Anjali nodded in agreement. 'I checked, and there's a flight to Bhubaneswar tomorrow. I'll book the tickets.'

Meenakshi added, 'Let's make sure we have everything we need.

Research materials, the map, and the amulets for protection.'

As they discussed their strategy, Meenakshi, always stays alert to all the current events, checked her phone for any news related to Jagannath Puri. Suddenly, her eyes widened in surprise.

'Guys, listen to this! The Ratna Bhandar of Jagannath Temple is going to be opened this Sunday, July 14,' Meenakshi announced, her voice filled with excitement.'

'Ratna Bhandar?' Sidhant questioned. 'What's that?'

Meenakshi quickly pulled up more information.

'The Ratna Bhandar is a treasure vault within the Jagannath Temple complex. It's one of the most secretive and heavily guarded places in the temple. Let me tell you the details.'

'The Ratna Bhandar is positioned within the inner sanctum zone of the shrine, which is the most scared section that houses the deities. Access is through the Bhogamandapa, used for making and offering food to these mighty gods. It has tight security, with entry limited to few priests and temple leaders. The public can't catch a glimpse, as it is opened on very rare occasions.'

Sidhant leaned in, intrigued. 'So, what's inside?'

Meenakshi continued, 'The Ratna Bhandar consists of seven chambers, each with specific functions and increasing levels of security. Here's a quick breakdown:

1. First Chamber, Its Entry point is used for storing items for daily rituals.

2. Second Chamber it contains ceremonial items, including some jewels.

3. Third Chamber holds silver and gold jewelry for the deities during festivals.

4. Fourth Chamber helps to store gems and precious stones.

5. Fifth Chamber houses contain the most valuable and rare jewels.

6. Sixth Chamber this stores the ceremonial attires and accessories of the deities.

7. Seventh Chamber, the innermost chamber, believed to contain the most sacred and ancient treasures, seldom opened and shrouded in mystery.'

'The treasures inside are donations and offerings collected over centuries from various kings, nobles, and devotees. These include gold, silver, diamonds, and other precious gems. There are numerous legends, one claiming that the vault contains a rare and powerful gem with mystical properties linked to divine protection and blessings.'

Anjali's eyes lit up with interest. 'So, there's a possibility that our gem could be in there?'

Meenakshi nodded. 'It's a strong lead. Especially since the vault is rarely opened, and this Sunday might be our only chance to access it.'

'Because of its invaluable contents, the Ratna Bhandar is under constant surveillance and protection. The exact contents are unknown to the public, which adds to its mystique. This makes it an ideal place to hide a piece of our gem. Legends also say that there are not just one but 52 Ratna Bhandar '

'Fifty-two? That's an insane number! How on earth are we supposed to find our gem hidden among so many chambers? And even if we do, how will we know which one is the right one?'

Anjali, ever the voice of reason, remained composed.

'We'll figure it out, Sidhant. There must be clues scattered throughout the temple or in the ancient scriptures. We've made it this far, and with everything we've learned, I'm confident we can do this.'

Meenakshi was staring at her amulet intently as she completed her work. Her eyes showed her curiosity and tenderness. Its nine-armed Goddess Durga's symbol, engraved on that particular amulet captivated her fully.

'This amulet... it feels so familiar. I've seen it before, but I can't recall when or where,' she says.

Sidhant, intrigued by her words, glances over at Anjali. 'By the way, Anjali, where's your amulet?'

Anjali, who had been quietly listening, replies, 'I've kept it in my bag.'

Sidhant frowns slightly. 'You should keep it close to you. It's for your safety, after all.'

Meenakshi nods in agreement, still holding her amulet. As she turns to Anjali, her eyes narrow as she notices something on Anjali's hand. 'What's this?' she asks, suddenly grabbing Anjali's hand. A burn mark, red and raw, stands out on Anjali's skin.

'How did you get this?'

Anjali hesitates before answering, 'It happened yesterday... I didn't want to bother you guys with it.'

Meenakshi's eyes flash with concern. 'You should have told us! This doesn't look like a normal burn. It's strange, almost too fresh.'

Sidhant, looking over Anjali's shoulder, nods in agreement.

'She's right. Normal burns don't look like that. Are you sure everything's okay?'

Anjali sighs. 'I actually rubbed my hand by mistake, that's why it looks like this.'

Meenakshi, still concerned, pulls out some medicine from her bag and gently applies it to Anjali's burn.

'You need to take care of yourself. We can't afford to have anything happen to you.'

Anjali smiles softly, appreciating the concern.

## Chapter 10

# The Enigmatic Map

The next day, they took off from their flight to Bhubaneswar. Their journey felt like a new chapter in their adventure. When they landed, the humid air of the city welcomed them and a hurry started brewing. Cutting short their stayed at the hotel and went on to do some preliminary research.

After getting settled in the hotel, Sidhant called someone quickly. 'Aarya will be here shortly," he says turning around to take a look at Meenakshi and Anjali 'she is an old friend who used to be part of some research team. She is unbelievably good-hearted as well as her family".

As they stepped out to meet Aarya, the temple's towering spires loomed in the distance, a constant reminder of their mission. Soon, Aarya arrived, her cheerful demeanor instantly putting everyone at ease.

'Hi! It's so nice to meet you both,' Aarya greeted, her smile warm and genuine.

'Likewise!' Meenakshi responded, exchanging a look with Anjali, both feeling an immediate connection with her.

As they walked to Aarya's home, she pointed towards the temple.

'My house is right near the Jagannath Temple. You can see the temple clearly from my room. Sidhant told me about your research. You're looking into the hidden artifacts of the Ratna Bhandar, right?'

Meenakshi nodded, slightly tense but relieved that Aarya seemed to know only the basics.

'Yes, just exploring some old legends,' Meenakshi said, trying to keep it vague.

Aarya's family, Pramod and Pragya, welcomed them with open arms.

The house was homely, adorned with tapestries while spices was wafting through the air. The sound of their laughter mingled with that of clanking dishes which created an environment that was very comfortable for all of them.

As they gathered at the breakfast table, a feast fit for kings awaited them with fluffy parathas, golden brown aloo sabzi, steaming chai.

It was like words flew out of everyone's mouth as even Pramod went ahead to share some funny stories from his child days as Pragya supplied recent deeds from where she lived.

There was something about this gathering which made Aarya think back on times gone past as she listened to her parents' voices filling the room as if it was not also meant to be filling stomachs with food that matched these tastes were likewise found on

memories lost, there was warmth radiating within walls leading up towards roof above this gathering including sun rays shining through windows.

'So, how long are you planning to stay?' Pragya asked, her eyes filled with curiosity.

'Not too long,' Sidhant answered politely. 'We just need to do some research, and then we'll be heading back.'

Aarya chimed in, 'Feel free to stay as long as you need. We love having guests, especially those who are friends of Sidhant.'

After breakfast, Aarya led them to a spacious room at the back of the house.

'This room should be perfect for your research. No one will disturb you here,' Aarya assured them.

'And if you need anything, don't hesitate to call me.'

As Aarya turned to leave, Meenakshi's gaze was caught by something on the wall. Her heart skipped a beat as she stared at a map.

'Wait,' she whispered, drawing closer to it. 'Look at that map!'

Sidhant and Anjali hurried over. 'What is it?' Anjali asked, noticing the intensity in Meenakshi's eyes.

'It's almost identical to the map we have,' Meenakshi said, pointing to a section of the map.

'But there's a difference—this one shows a tunnel!'

'A tunnel?' Sidhant echoed in surprise , he was evident in his voice. 'How did we miss that?'

Meenakshi turned to Aarya, who had stopped in the doorway, sensing their urgency. 'Aarya, where did you find this map?'

Aarya stepped back into the room, her brows furrowed in thought. 't's been ages since I discovered it in the course of my study about the shrine. There was reference to an underground passage that fascinated me but I have always been unable to find any sign of its existence whatsoever, no matter what I did.'

'Why didn't you tell me about this before?' Sidhant asked, a mix of excitement and concern in his voice.

Aarya shrugged slightly.

'I didn't think much of it since the tunnel seemed to be just a rumor. But now that you mention it, maybe it's worth looking into.'

Meenakshi exchanged a look with Sidhant and Anjali.

'This could be the clue we've been searching for. If the tunnel exists, it might lead us to the hidden chambers of the Ratna Bhandar.'

Anjali nodded, her mind racing with possibilities. 'We should explore this as soon as possible.'

The air in Aarya's room felt thick with tension, and everyone could sense it. Meenakshi's gaze was locked on the map, her thought process working overtime. Aarya could feel the intensity creeping in, so she spoke.

Aarya tilted her head a bit.

'Gem? Which gem are you all talking about?' she questioned, clearly perplexed.

Meenakshi was ready to respond but Anjali interrupted.

'Well, we aren't entirely sure about that,' she remarked to ease the tension. 'It is just said to be some very precious– highly valuable, one of a kind, something like that.'

Aarya still looked mildly confused but started to nod her head slowly as if something Aarya just remembered had come to her.

Anjali directed her attention back to Meenakshi as if attempting to steer the topic elsewhere.

'So, Meenakshi, that terrible looking old book, where on earth did you get that from?' she asked, gesturing at the large dusty aged book sitting in the center of the table.

Meenakshi gently caressed the old cover of the book.

'I've had it for a long time,' she said. 'I didn't pay much attention to it previously, but when we were about to assemble the pieces, I realized there could be a few pointers in it. That is why I carried it with me.'

Sidhant, who had been mostly quiet throughout this part of the conversation, interjected. 'And I suspect that pointer is taking us straight to Gundicha Temple.'

Aarya's eyebrows shot up. 'Gundicha Temple? What does that have to do with any of this?' she asked, obviously confused.

Meenakshi offered reassurance that was both soothing and assertive at the same time. 'I saw something on the map, Aarya it's the Navagraha Mandala,' Meenakshi began. A figure of eight wrench associated with Hindu and the nine planets. As such, the Gundicha Temple is of a religious site which is devoted to Lord

Jagannath during the annual Ratha Yatra procession . However, it also possesses metaphysical aspects that go deeper than what most are aware of.'

Anjali cut in, glancing among the audience. 'Navagraha has developed over the years. It theory was that it was use for tracking activities on earth such as eclipses, tides, even monarchy systems. There was a more interesting aspect of this however and that was about tales of its being a guardian or sealing away something or cover entry.'

Sidhant gave a slight spin to his head. 'That's right. Also, the Gundicha Temple embedded in the path of Lord Jagannath has its pilgrimage history and stands to reasons that it must be the place where this buried entrance the tunnel begins.'

Aarya, who was still trying to wrap her brains around the idea, posed a question, 'But how did you relate it to Gundicha Temple? I am not getting it.'

Meenakshi smiled thinly. 'You need to look at the map again,' she said while indicating a part of the sculpture that illustrated the Navagraha Mandala. "The temple is central to all of this. The secret is in the structure of the Navagraha, its placement and the placement of the respective temples. And with regards to that, it corresponds to the alignment of the Gundecha Temple. This is where the tunnel is most likely concealed.'

Aarya was now completely focused. 'So you mean the temple is at the center of the Navagraha Mandala which directs the temple and there is a secret tunnel below the temple?'

Meenakshi nodded her head appreciatively. 'Yes, that tunnel might very well help us reach the Devi Bimala temple. But not the typical Devi Bimala temple which you can imagine. This temple borders on the Asuras.'

Finished Anjali in a more serious manner. 'There are tales that the Devi temple keeps something of great value save for her or behind her. The treasure perhaps. Still, a daunting task awaits. The Asuras will not allow even a toddler near it without some bloodshed.'

Aarya's eyes widened again. 'Asuras? Are those the demon-like figures that are portrayed in the stories in the Hindu culture?'

Sidhant nodded gravely. 'Yes, those. And if the legend is to be believed, then these are not just any demons. These ones guard a precious stone and only the ones deemed worthy are allowed to access it.'

Aarya was now leaning back, overwhelmed but intrigued.

'This is all so... unbelievable.'

Meenakshi sighed. 'I know. But everything we've seen, everything we've uncovered, points to this. We have to follow the trail and if we can find the gem, maybe... just maybe, we'll be able to solve the mystery.'

The room fell silent as the weight of what they were about to undertake pressures them down

# Chapter 11

# The Lost Path to the Hidden Treasure

Aarya sat down; her voice almost resigned.

'So, let me get this straight. There's a hidden tunnel under the Gundicha Temple which is protected by ancient celestial deities, and we need to figure out when the stars align to even stand a chance of finding this treasure?'

Sidhant smiled faintly. 'Pretty much.'

Aarya shook her head. 'You three are totally insane.'

Anjali laughed softly. 'You're with us now, welcome to the madness.'

Meenakshi's fingers followed the contours of the map her head leaning forward unable to think.

Meenakshi took a deep breath and spoke further 'The Navagraha is not any simple arrangement of figures. It is not just an illustration of the planets in the sky. It is a solution, an answer to the question'

Aarya threw a glance at her and her expression scrunched with bewilderment.

'The Navagraha? As in the nine planets? What does this have that got to do with the temple or... anything at all?'

Meenakshi replied in a slow nod, a dawning understanding igniting in her eyes.

'Yes, the nine gods of the Navagraha are the Sun, the Moon, Mars, Mercury, Jupiter, Venus, and Saturn and the Rahu and Ketu all laid out here in this circular pattern. The structure of the Gundecha Temple and its surroundings was not an arbitrary design. It was built in alignment with the Navagraha Mandala. The structure of the temple with its concepts of foundation and elevation were established when the planets were in a favorable position. It links the territorial and the heavenly spheres.'

Sidhant leaned over the table on the map.

'You mean to say that the layout of the temple follows the design of the Nine planets? But what does that do for us exactly? Are we looking for a secret entrance or something of that sort?'

Meenakshi to her credit maintained her composure. 'Yes, precisely. Such a tunnel will only be reachable when these planets occupy that position once more, or we have a precise relation to them. It is a space-time vortex or a cosmic aperture.'

Aarya's brow was still knitted.

'However, how do we link this to the gem? You all always talk about it' she said.

Meenakshi tried to explain but Anjali interjected first.

'...Not quite, but it's something we believe is hidden somewhere in the temple and would be hard to find. It's something that is very old and connected to the history of the temple.'

Aarya scanned the rest of the group in absolute bewilderment. 'Important in what way? What is so extraordinary about that one?'

A soft smile crept onto Anjali's face to ease the ongoing pressure. 'It is expected to be highly valued – perhaps not necessarily monetarily, but otherwise. We'll know it in a short while.'

Meenakshi explained, 'Navagraha stands for the nine planetary elements which are related to different functionalities and spheres of existence. It is regarded as highly sacred in ancient Vedic history and precise science of temple architecture. Numerous temples, like the ones in Puri, for example, were erected after the sky.'

Aarya frowned in puzzlement. 'But how is this related to the Gundicha Temple?'

Meenakshi felt forward, her voice brimming with excitement from the insight.

'The Navagraha can be found in several scriptures. These nine planetary bodies find a place at appropriate locations within the temple design. Each planet rules over a certain corner and section of the temple's energies. I was looking at the temple's plans, and in fact, I found that there is a secret position of the Gundecha temple's main shrine in relation to those planets. It is as though the entire temple is designed in such a way that it functions like a clock and its powers can only be unleashed upon the correct alignment of the Navagraha.'

Anjali approvingly turned her head toward Meenakshi.

'And that alignment is important too, when looking for the tunnel's entry.'

Meenakshi wore a smile. 'That is right. The concealed tunnel's entry point lies underneath the main temple courtyard near the rest house for the divine idols before and after the Ratha Yatra ceremony. This tunnel is very old, and the sad thing is that only those capable of comprehending the role of Navagraha can navigate the proper way into it. The navigation system based on the stars has a grounding feature in this temple as well as the spiritual one.'

Sidhant's look expressed disorientation.

'So… this tunnel is closed or concealed because the stars are positioned somewhere?'

Meenakshi understood the confusion. 'Not quite. The opening has always existed but has suffered from neglect for hundreds of years. The symbols of the Navagraha are written as instructions and such a route can only be shown by those who know the planets and their ways.'

As soon as the party walks into the Gundecha Temple, one can sense an overpowering presence of history within the precinct, almost as if their innumerable enigmas were lurking within the walls waiting to be deciphered. The stone walls are engraved with artistic designs that looked as if they have Sunset years of history behind them. Aarya, Anjali, Meenakshi, and Sidhant remain motionless gazing at the enormous temple structure.

Out of the blue, Anjali observes something strange embedded in one of the stone walls. There is a three-dimensional, prism-like sculpture located in the middle of a carved star navy. She goes a bit further, her finger grazing the hard cold stone.

'What…is this?' Anjali finally asks after some silence.

Everyone steps in and at some point, Aarya's face comes into view as she certainly examines something. The so-called prism is actually not a simple ornament—it appears to emit a faint sparkle reflecting any light present within the temple.

Anjali proceeds in, 'This isn't merely some decoration. This suffers over here,' she points to the structure.

'It's embedded into the stone in a manner which seems like it is aimed to catch the light from the moon directly.'

Meenakshi's eyes go wide and she understands. This is what she says, part of the hidden star map. It's designed like that, to catch the light of the moon and hide something behind it. I've seen this in books—there is a technique which is used in these temples where the moon light passes through a prism and illuminates a clear path or in other words rather map along a section of the temple.

Aarya grimaces, still at a loss. 'But what does this have to do with Navagraha?'

Meenakshi withdraws slightly, speaking to herself. 'Navagraha—the nine planets—and their goddesses are in charge of the universe. This device appears to be under their dominion, particularly the moon. There is a specific angle at which light from the particular moon will hit this prism, and for the first time ever, appear on the surface of the ground or wall marking the place where the entrance of the tunnel lies.'

Sharpening his style of conversation with an intrigue quote, Sidhant looked quite pleased. 'So, what you are trying to say is, we need to wait for the moonlight to hit this exact point?"

'Exactly,' Meenakshi nods. 'The reflection will guide us to the hidden entrance. I'm sure of it.'

# Chapter 12

# The star map

Once the group steps into the precincts of the Gundicha Temple, a feel of sanctity emerges all around. The granite walls were appearing as if they are full of life, while inscribed each of the block carried the tale of several hundred years. This temple is not as elaborately designed as the towering Jagannath Temple, but there is a sense of magic in the simplicity of the temple, as if one would appreciate the beauty of the temple better if one knew more about it. Every stone seems like a history book that is pulsating with life.

Aarya feels as though time has come to a standstill as she inspects deeper into the temple. She feels a sense of time slowing down as she steps further into the temple. The wide courtyard is soundless, and the subtle scent of incense lingers in the air, remnants of long-past rituals filled the place with a sense of divinity.

Meenakshi again comes to the halt, examining the elaborately carved depictions that adorned the walls – the glorious stories of the deities, chiefly, Lord Jagannath, and those of the nine planets or Navagraha, carved onto the temple's poles.

The floor is made of stone and is comfortably warm, it has been worn down and smoothed by the feet of the countless devotees who have navigated this particular path before them.

With Anjali's wide eye exploring the area, she also looks up at the high ceiling with the old stone beams that hold the very structure in place.

'It feels... timeless,' she muses, her voice almost a whisper, as if the words would disrupt the sacred silence.

'As if something's waiting.'

A slight breeze flows through the corridors while in the distance a light rustling voice echoes as if it is heard though the very surfaces of the room. Through small openings, light shines into the edifice, illuminating the inner part of the temple, which is yearly occupied by Lord Jagannath, during the Ratha Yatra, at the very back of the temple.

All at once, Anjali notices an image— a colorful prism-like shape that is fixed inside the rock. It is almost conspicuous since it has almost blend with the manifold sculptures of gods and heaven ornaments.

'Where?' Anjali is already pointing, bringing everyone's attention towards it.

'This… is not like what we have seen.'

Meenakshi walks closer, squinting her eyes.

'This is the place where the moonlight has to come in,' she says in a hushed tone.

'It's a concealed apparatus – something quite old, a chart of the stars.'

The realization sets in - 'The fact dawns on them, this was not merely a place of worship. It was a lock and *a map in a possession*. It was now clear how moon light would come through the tiny openings carved in the walls of the temple tracing a hidden path on the temple floor, revealing the way forward.'

But while they miss the light from the heavens down, Aarya finds herself thinking about the tales of the Navagraha. 'Isn't it likely that under those nine deities and their alignment was also constructed the passageway currently located below the floor? Or was the map made as these planets were aligned to possess this cosmic power that had kept a certain gold treasure entrance secret buried under layers of history?'

Anjali suddenly looked up; her eyes wide were with realization. 'Guys, we need to hurry up. Today is 16th October!'

Meenakshi, still deep in thought, looked confused.

'Okay, but what's so special about that?'

Sidhant glanced at Anjali, his brow furrowing.

'Anjali, are you saying this because today is Sharada Purnima?'

'Yes, exactly!' Anjali exclaimed.

'Tonight is Sharada Purnima, the night when the moon's shine will be at its absolute peak. It's the best time for the tunnel to be unlocked.'

Meenakshi gasped, suddenly remembering.

'Oh my God, you're right! I almost forgot. The light from the moon reflecting through the prisms will be strongest tonight. We have to act fast!'

Sidhant nodded, urgency creeping into his voice.

'If we miss this, we might not get another chance for a long time.'

The group exchanged tense looks, each of them realizing that time was running out. They needed to act now, or risk losing their only chance.

Meenakshi could feel her heart beat run faster as they are all silent, contemplating the essence of Sharada Purnima. The atmosphere surrounding them felt different. It felt heavy, charged, and filled with the energy of yore. Outside the window all of them glanced it was almost the close of the day.

'I am losing my patience! The moon will shine the brightest by the end of the day. This is the last dip before the next Sharada Purnima,' came Anjali's voice which was a bit shaky with anticipation.

Sidhant, who was usually calm, did not seem so, as if he too was beginning to feel that something around them was stirring. He turned his eyes to the map on the table. 'If the stories correspond,' he started, 'the hidden star map can only reveal itself when the moon is at its zenith on this night. The reflection from the temple stones will guide us'

Meenakshi's mind spun in motion. She could not have conceived it; the mere notion of a concealed star map which will be only visible when the moon casts its rays upon it sounded utterly fictional and yet this was the reality, they found themselves standing at the border of a entire new sphere, pushing forward solely on the basis of intuition and sparse ancient hints available to them.

While they all remained quiet and looked at each other, there was silence until Anjali choked out 'OH !'

'The stones! The ones I earlier mentioned in the Gundecha temple ... the prism shaped ones! If everything falls into place and the moon would shine perfectly on them tonight, they should be able to project the concealed map onto the temple's surface.'

'No, I mean, draw it because it's not a physical one, it's a conjuncture of some other thing,' Sidhant looked at them in comprehension

'That's it! The stars did not only create a physical path - the tunnel was not only a tunnel - it is a celestial tunnel leading us to the unknown.'

When the storm passed, Meenakshi carefully nodded her head.

'In that case, we have to hurry up. The tunnel entrance can be located using that star map, provided we make it to the temple before it is too late.'

There was a thrill in the atmosphere of the room each second was crucial.

The thought of the star map being reflected by prism-shaped stones had raised yet another aspect of the enigma.

Anjali sat up straighter with curiosity, 'What if the temple serves more than just as a place of worship? What if behind it lies the worlds key which allows us the access to something that is not visible to any average person?'

Meenakshi looked at the map again and said softly.

'The temple all along has had several features associating it with stars and other celestial bodies.

They say, that healthy line separating the divine from the earthly is at its weakest during the Sharada Purnima festival. If we follow the moonlit... it should take us directly to the door.'

The faintest winds howled from beyond the window, shaking trees causing the whole night to feel even more alive. There was no more point in wasting the time. Meenakshi seized the map, and without any further communication, they all stepped outside, the cold air burning as they ran through the dark night.

The night possessed an eerie calmness, a calm that was not just a reference but a danger sign as Meenakshi, Sidhant and Anjali along with Aarya huddled in Aarya's room working on the last bits before embarking on the unknown journey.

The tension in the air was both anxious and irritating as Aarya produced a map and her fingers traced the path to the archaeological shrine known as the Gundecha Temple.

'We have only a window of one hour,' Aarya reminded them in a commanding tone.

'The temple will only be accessible between the hours of three and four in the morning. If we don't make it in time…'

She trailed off but it was clear to them what she meant. If that time was lost, it would be the end of the road and they will have to wait for one-month more which is not possible as they have to get the gem before the Asura.

The packings started after such brief hesitations and were completed packing every item that was there and due to be there Anjali the most pragmatic of them all, checked the flashlights and the rope again and again. Sidhant, the one with boundless curiosity, toyed with an old map Aarya had found a couple of weeks back. As for Meenakshi, she kept her eyes glued to the amulet she wore, whose mysterious engravings illuminated weakly in the darkness.

# Chapter 13

# A letter from the unknown

A shrill cry rang out, breaking the silence and drawing everyone's attention. They turned to the window to see a giant eagle sitting there with piercing blue eyes like they had never seen before. The eagle held a scroll in its claws that was closed with a seal that none of them knew.

'It appears to be a letter,' announced Sidhant, who barely raised his voice albeit afraid it might disturb the fragile air that filled the room.

The eagle dropped the letter on the window sill and gave out another eerie cry before it vanished into the dark sky. Meenakshi extended her hand to the letter whilst a chill ran down her spine and her hands slightly shook.

The impressions on the seal made it look like a symbol of an Ouroboros enclosed in a circle of some arcane language.

Thinking about the others without the seal, Meenakshi took a sigh and unfurled the scroll.

The message included enciphered directions which were written in an unfamiliar to them all language. Some symbols Meenakshi deciphered as part of the intricate design present on the amulet she carried with her, and as such understanding dawned upon her.

'This is concern with the amulet,' she said in a tone barely above whisper yet with an assured conviction. 'These are the instructions ... on how to work this.

'But how?' Anjali leant in to look at the letter, which Sidhant was still holding, and asked in her sweetest voice. 'What do we do?'

The content of the letter was obscure it only referred to several details such as moonlight, reflection, and an old carving portrayed within the Gundecha Temple. Meenakshi's gaze scanned the letter in streaks, piecing her mind together as images filled her head. A million queries danced in her head but the most important aspect was there was no way out, the only way was through the clues.

'We'll cross that bridge when we get to it,' Sidhant said, forcing what he hoped was a brave face. But it was the outpouring of a voice that was shaken.

They were stepping into the void; it was true that they had been ready for this fielding for weeks, yet the nature of the danger that lay ahead was starting to dawn on them.

As they proceeded with their packing, an unspoken understanding lingered between them. It was clear to them that this task wasn't merely resolving old enigmas but dangerous. If the Asura were to retrieve the stone before them, it would be curtains.

There was a great deal of tension in the air as they polished the last details of their plans.

A burden of the moment was pressuring them, and the passing of time was now painfully sharp since the scheduled time was approaching. Meenakshi's held enveloped believing the letter is talking about the amulet, as she wished - as she believed - that it was the right decision.

## Chapter 14

# The Amulet's Secret

The team felt that it was important to get the blessings of the gods first before they were to embark on the perilous journey. Meenakshi felt guilt-ridden for having stepped into the temple under such circumstances, and that made her feel sad.

Upon arriving at the Jagannath Temple, they stood facing the idols of Lord Jagannath, Baladeva, Subhadra, Bimala Devi, and Vishvanath and offered some prayers without words. Meenakshi's eyes welled with tears at the sheer beauty and majesty of the Deities.

Sidhant saw her inhibition and placed a hand on her shoulder for support. 'Meenakshi, we have positive reasons to engage in these activities. We are doing this to avoid a bigger calamity. This is the will of the gods. We need to focus on recovering the gem before the Asura does.'

Meenakshi nodded in agreement this time, and after one last bow, the members of the group stepped outside the temple feeling more motivated, and ready to take the challenge.

As the group walked into the ancient temple, they came to a halt. Bright beams of the moonlight fell on a large prismatic object that was suspended from the ceiling and it focused the light on one place at the ground, illuminating the stone surface very brightly.

The square portion of the floor that the light fell on looked quite normal, which only left everyone confused.

'What I want to know is where the door is.' Aarya inquired, sounded more impatient than before even in a whisper.

Sidhant squinted at the pigeon spot on the ground. 'It must be over here. There must be something underneath it.'

Meenakshi scoured the stone wall, caressing its fine antiquities, looking for some hint or mechanism. She had an unsettling sense they overlooked something. As she stepped out towards the wall, Anjali carelessly collided against her making Meenakshi lose her footing. As she fell down, Anjali let out a little scream.

'Careful!' Sidhant reproved, even if his tone was light. But the tumble had something unexpected caused—Meenakshi's attention was caught by a detailed figure of a goddess.

Her fingers wandered upon it and her heart skipped a beat when she sensed something odd. It felt like there was a tiny piece of the sculpture that was absent.

'Stop!' Meenakshi shouted, filled with enthusiasm. 'There's something here.'

Anjali, annoyed yet interested, stood back in the circle and brushed off her clothes as others came towards her.

'What is it?' Anjali inquired.

Meenakshi indicated the area in the wall carving where a piece was missing.

'Something's supposed to go in there. I have a feeling that this could be our answer.'

Anjali's face brightened with understanding. 'Give me the letter.'

Meenakshi passed the letter to Anjali, who read it briefly, then froze. 'The poem says,

*Upon the neck, a secret lies,*

*In ancient stone where silence cries,*

*The goddess spoke, but who can hear?*

*A key in gold, the path unclears.*

*Turn the thread where shadows sleep,*

*A hidden lock, the secret deep,*

*The stars may guide, the light may bend,*

*Yet who can see where paths descend?*

*The moon does glance, the prism plays,*

*In shifting sands and endless maze,*

*The shape you seek is not in sight,*

*But in your hand, it holds the light.*

*A symbol worn, a mystery cold,*

*What stories in the metal fold?*

*The answer waits, beyond the veil,*

*A truth unlocked by hand so frail.*

If we analyze this properly it is talking about the amulet,'

Aarya broke the rest of the silence and exclaimed 'Amulet? What amulet'

'It's a really long story we will tell you about it later' Siddhant assured Aarya

Sidhant and Anjali directed their gazes at Meenakshi, their eyes growing large at the same time.

Without thinking, she held onto the charm that she had worn around her neck for most of her life—the amulet given by the guardian. It felt strange, Meenakshi's amulet was different from the other's amulet from the very start Aarya's gaze brightened with joy. 'This one is for you, Meenakshi. The amulet is the key.'

Immediately, Meenakshi took off her amulet and inserted it into the round on the wall. The small Durga symbol on the amulet slotted well into the empty space.

There was a faint noise all over. The stone screed where the beam of light had fallen began to move, level by level. One segment of the scrubbed section of the floor appeared like a trap door, was let up to reveal another hidden staircase.

Meenakshi nearly took out the amulet, and Sidhant wasted no effort. He made his forward and yanked the trapdoor completely, exposing steep stairs leading down into the dimness which were made out of stones.

'Come,' he spoke, and at that point, they went down without saying anything else.

The flight of stairs led to a faintly lit hallway, at the end of which the group faced a large aged door. The pair of the doors had beautiful engravings of legendary animals and deities crafted on them. They noticed a small keyhole at the center of the door with its artistic designs.

He inhaled deeply. 'A door ... again? What do you expect we should do about this one?'

Meenakshi's face clouded with concentration. She once more made a move toward her amulet, feeling the surface of it. Somewhere within her, she knew that this time things would be different.

At the rear of the object, her fingers touched a fine filament. A swift pull opened a hidden section that contained a small, decorative key.

'Looks like it worked,' Meenakshi spoke in total awe and relief.

After she turned the key in the lock, the door opened with a soft sound and immediately a rush of air announced the action – the door opened – and the mysteries behind it introduced themselves...

# Chapter 15

# Unveiling the first gem

As the team walks into the breath taking, perfumed room, the Kumkum Chandan scent fills the room as walk in. It has the very smell of the goddess herself. Their gaze then immediately fixes on the sculpture, well-adorned with dazzling stones that are almost alive and greatly enhancing the beauty of the Goddess.

A stone at the topmost position of the crown worn by the Devi Bimala resonates with spectacular luminescence thanks to the flattering moonlight that beams down in it, and illumines the very arena in which it is placed.

Before them at the feet of the goddess, there is a pot in the shape of lotus with another bright shining uncut diamond set within. Mesmerized by its beauty, Meenakshi hurries to touch it. Just then, as she was about to touch it, the situation changes.

Behind them, there was the sound of hurried thumping footsteps that was aggressive and heavy that made the group cower in fear. They quickly look back only to face the Asuras, who were wielding sharp swords and were looking down on them with threats.

Suddenly, Anjali, Sidhant, and Aarya are grabbed and held and swords are placed at their necks so that the cold metal touches their skin.

Meenakshi, who managed to hold on the precious stone, holds it firmly as her heart raced, promising herself that she would not release it. However, the evil sounding deep voices of the Asuras filled the room and made their hearts faint.

One of the Asura menaces, 'Give us the gemstone perhaps we will grant you a swifter death. But today, all of you will perish.'

As the Asura strides from behind towards Meenakshi, his sword held precariously close to her neck, he boasts,

'It is not time yet to die, but to witness the death of your friends, I will kill you soon enough.'

This makes Meenakshi shed tears as she prays for help from Goddess Bimala in silence. During this time, one tear falls from her eye and drips onto the jewel she is holding. Just then, when the Asura attempts to touch the gem, it erupts in a luminous light that is blinding and dazzling.

The Asuras let out sharp cries that are unbearably loud and high-pitched as they attempt to escape, but their efforts fail. As the powers of the gem's divinity envelop the Asuras, their figures lose form within the bright light and dissolve into thin air.

The ensuing stillness is almost palpable, as the animated group begins to open their eyes one by one with a heavy presence of panting.

Aarya is blank with confusion while as for Meenakshi, who is still shaking, places her hands to the idol of the goddess in pure relief. She offers a short prayer thanking them as they would indeed be dead without them.

When she comes back to herself, still feeling stunned and shaken,

Aarya utters, 'What's ... has just occurred? Is it as though I am dreaming? How come this is happening and where are you people concealing?' Scared and disoriented, he says the latter with a quivering voice'

Drawing close, Anjali covers his shoulder, 'This isn't the perfect occasion, Aarya. We'll clarify everything, but not in this place. We have to first return home.'

Sidhant shakes his head, 'We cannot afford to leave just yet.'

Aarya, looking at his wrist, dramatically states, 'But it's already 5 in the morning! The morning aarti has surely commenced. We can't go out and come back the same way.'

Pacing back and forth in a salient manner, Aarya goes on to say, 'So are you saying that we have to remain cooped up for one more day?'

Composed again, Meenakshi holds, 'There has to be a different way out.'

The group climbs up the stairs to check the trapdoor through which they had come in – it is bolted. Sidhant pulls at it, still it does not move.

Anjali, sounding irritated, says, 'There should be another way out. It must be around this place.'

They go back to the main room of the temple, exploring it bit by bit.

At first, they do not see anything odd to this, until they start sweeping the room with their gaze, and focus on the four tall pillars situated at each corner of the room.

On further observation, they realize that each of the pillars has something on top and intricate designs carved upon it.

# Chapter 16

# Discoveries and Dangers

In the end, after visiting all the different places over there, the group found themselves back in the room, even more puzzled as to the purpose of their visit - how to get out of the temple.

Until the notices that each of the four corners of the temple had stone pillars. On each pillar, the name of a goddess was written, however, the statues that were located under them looked rather suspicious.

The first pillar had a statue of an owl and the name of goddess named Manasa Devi was caved, who is known for her powers as a snake avenger. The second pillar read Shail Putri, although a snake was present at the base. On the third one, a cow's idol was placed while the name Shashthi was portrayed on it. The fourth pillar was caved as Lakshmi however, a cat's idol was placed.

Sidhant, who came near to the carvings suggested,

'This does not make sense. This arrangement seems to be off. Look at the vahana of the goddesses. If I am right, Manasa Devi rides a snake, not an owl. Shail Putri rides a snake and not a cow. Whereas, Devi Shashthi is never ever seen with a cow but rather with a cat, right? And the last one, it is stated that Lakshmi's vahana is an owl, not a cat.'

'Ah,' Aarya understood him and gave an additional

'So, basically, what you mean to say is there is a misplacement of the idols and we need to fix them in the correct order,' nodding her head to show that his guess was right and Sidhant agreed and under everyone's assistance, they commenced hanging the idols again.

Cut off from their usual focus and attentive hacks, Meenaakshi steadfastly moved the snake on Manasa Devi's pillar while Aarya changed the position of the cow from Shail Putri. Anjali kept the cat with Devi Shashthi and Sidhant placed the owl under the statue of Lakshmi.

The instant the final idol was adjusted, an eerie sound reverberated through the air as if the stone pillars themselves were shifting. The idol, along with the stone pillars, submerged, thereby extending a recess to the group.

'What say after all this?' she said in a low voice full of apprehension.

Then the noise died into the nothingness of peace. A door behind them opened slowly to reveal a dark room with a staircase that was leading upward. Sidhant looked into the dark space and stopped breathing as they heard the distant wind calling through the tunnel.

'There's our way out,' he said, indicating the stairs.

They felt relieved but still careful as they started to climb. As they went higher, the light from their torches began to dim and finally quenched, enclosing them in total darkness.

Meenakshi wheezed and lunged for the others. 'Hands together,' she hissed.

In the midst of the darkness, they interlocked, resolutely depending on one another. They advanced slowly in hope that the goddess would lead them. At last, just when they were almost at the bottom of the stairs, a dim light could be seen and the audience experienced a sense of relief.

## Chapter 17

# A Slippery Escape

Once they approached the last step of the staircase, Meenakshi took action stepping forward, but with caution.

'I believe we are almost free—' However, before she finished speaking, the floor began to cave in, and let out a shrill scream, the four of them started to fall down a concealed tunnel, their cries reflecting against the stone walls.

'AHHHHH! I am the First to fall off the Edge, swinging my hands in all directions. 'THIS ISN'T A PART OF THE ROLLER COASTER RIDE I TOOK.'

Anjali attempted to hold onto the edges but lost her grip and turned. 'This is more than my worst nightmare!' Aarya who was clutching Meenakshi was screaming for dear life.

They tumbled, flipped, wherever they were tossed until they were ejected off into a clear sky, where they landed with a resounding thud on a heap of branches and dirt. Their fall was broken by grass and climber plants but that didn't spare them from knocking against one another.

'Aa!' Meenakshi groaned as she came to the realization that she was squished in between Sidhant and Aarya.

'Can someone please stop lying on my hair?'

'Not until you take your elbow out of my side,' Sidhant complained as he tried to squirm out but ended up flopping on Anjali instead.

'I'm trapped!' Aarya moaned in an over-the-top manner; her face almost touching the dirt.

'I'm pretty sure I will perish in this position.'

'Calm down,' Anjali said, her head buried in a climber plant.

'The good thing is, at least the fall wasn't hard.'

At last, the group managed to free themselves of the entanglement and get out of the ground, shaking off the leaves and dust from their outfits. Aarya turned around and screamed.

'The slide! It's disappeared!'

Aarya's house was their last stop, and at that moment every muscle in their bodies was so tired they could not move, their legs were still quaking from the long, wild adventure.

They entered her room in a hurry and leaned against the wall with difficulty, their eyes darting all over the place, breathing hard, dead white yet still recovering from the shock of whatever it was that had just happened. There was no motion in the atmosphere but it was sizzling with some untamed spirit.

Meenakshi took a deep breath, her hands shaking a little from weariness, and opened her handbag. Slowly, she brought her hand back from that place and somewhere in the depths of the bag, a jewel appeared.

The very instant she held it in her hand, the very atmosphere of the chamber transformed completely. This was not a mere stone. The gem was beautifully luminous in the dim room and filled each and every inch of the space with soft light. It glowed and undulated in the colors of blue, as if divine energies were pouring through it. It even seemed to pulsate with a deep, resonant, almost heartbeat like thrum that emanated from its center.

They were all entranced. Aarya managed to speak after a short pause, and admonished, 'All right, now. Can someone kindly explain what on Earth just happened?'

Loud and deep yet gentle, the figure remarked, emerging out from a circular flaming portal

'Aha! I see you have discovered the jewel, my child.'

With a dazed look, Anjali managed to touch Meenakshi.

'We were going to tell you everything,' she said.

But Meenakshi, having snapped out of her stupor, looked up and faced the figure.

'If you possessed the key all these whiles, why did you not get the gem back yourself?'

The guardian, whose face was hidden in the depths of a hood, smiled graciously.

'The gem can only be accessed by the ones who are meant to, so that is why, it was easy for you to take in.'

Sidhant laughed, breathless. 'Easy? That was easy? For real?'

The guardian laughed; a deep, amused laugh that reached everyone present. 'In comparison to what is to come, yes... it was.'

Sidhant crossed his arms. 'But the Asura don't even get to touch the gem. They were defeated with it. So, that's no problem to worry about, right? They can't reach it.'

The guardian's smile lessened slightly.

'It is not that straightforward. Otherwise, we would not have come to you.'

Anjali moved forward, interested. 'And who are you really? You only said before that when we met you again, you would tell us everything.'

The guardian adjusted upright, the power in their eyes discernible through the hood.

'You are familiar with the fabled Shangri-La, are you not? Most say it is just an imagination, a tale of many centuries of the past, and yet it exists. We, the guardians, dwell in that place, keeping the secrets and the belongings of the deities safe.'

## Chapter 18

# The Hidden World's Calling

A heavy, oppressive sensation filled the air in the room, nearly viscous in its strangeness, as the three individuals remained transfixed by the silhouette in front of them. There was a distortion in the atmosphere, as if space and time did not exist for the man dressed in plain yet archaic garments.

Anjali was the first one to speak, even after anxious moments. She could feel the pounding in her chest. Her tongue felt as if it were glued to the roof of her mouth and her voice shook.

'Rishi... Kashyap? You... are one of the Saptrishi?'

The figure nodded with some gravity, the depth of his gaze displaying the ancient and boundless wisdom that his age could permit.

'Yes, is it not obvious? Kashyap I am the begetter of all—the serpents, Garuda, the asuras and the devatas.'

His voice was deep and steady, like thunder in the distance preceding the storm, carrying with it ages of existence.

So did Anjali's realization almost cripple her. Ordinary sages there were, but this was Rishi Kashyap the mighty, the ancient seer who gave birth to peoples and is one the Prominet Saptarishi.

'I... I can't believe this,' she said under her breath as amazement and terror battled inside her heart.

'You are he who begot all—Garuda and Naga?' Her voice trembled as his overbearing corporeality refused to compute in her frail mind.

Kashyap's face remained cool and calm as always. No emotion showed on his face.

'What you have learned are merely small parts of the whole story, my child.'

Meenakshi, who had not said a word until now, knelt before the venerable sage in prayer.

'How can us, simple human beings, help someone as mighty as you? What you, the Rishi Kashyap the one from who holds the universe is in his palm, need with us?'

Kashyap softened his gaze on her.

'And you think this is an easy thing I am attempting to do? If it was that simple, do you think I could have come looking for you? No, this is far much deeper than what you can understand

– this is the work of God, a task that is greater than you can ever bear.'

Then Sidhant, feeling the strange events from earlier, outburst, slightly perplexed.

'But... we don't have any powers. And why us? Why do you think we were chosen?'

The sage focused on him, his eyes sparkling with something that was both funny and sad.

'Your sight is only limited to the present sweet child but I, how do I put it in chronological perspective, have existed past and future. This is not just an apartment in the narrative of which you are a resident today. This is part of your very ancient existence.'

'Ancient existence?' Meenakshi's voice broke as she looked up, shocked by the information. 'What happened in our past life?'

Rishi Kashyap raised a finger. 'That is something that you will grasp surely but with time. For now, what is important for you to know, is that you are not here by accident. I failed to save you once in your previous lives, but I will not let the same fate befall you again. You are my children, and I will protect you.'

The three of them fell quiet for a moment, as they attempted to come to terms with the enormity of what they had just heard. There were elements in their lives they had no power over.

Kashyap went on, weaving words to form a steady line across the blank expanse of chaos threatening to take over their minds.

'The current assignment is to look for the temple and then bring back its sacred awe as well as the precious stone. This is the start of a longer expedition. The road above is perilous, full of unimaginable obstacles, but you will conquer if you do not waver.'

The seriousness of what he had said enveloped them like a blanket.

'But... where do we start?' Sidhant queried, which was still digesting the information.

'What do we have to do now?'

Kashyap's eyes shone with knowledge. 'Your next destination is Tara Tarini, one among the ten Mahavidya. Where her blessing Will take you further in the journey. Nothing will move without her grace. The stone that you are holding, Meenakshi,' he trailed as she reflexively caressed the pouch that was hanging from her shoulder,

'I shall keep safe for the time being. I will be the one to guarantee its security.'

Without a second thought, Meenakshi relinquished the gem, as though knowing it was only temporary, for the weight of responsibility...

'This journey,' Kashyap added as he placed the gem into his robes, 'is not only about this world. It is about the divine in the heavens. Every step you take will be subject to Divine Forces that you cannot control, but do not worry – we have the hand of the god above us.'

Sidhant couldn't calm himself down; his head was brimming with queries. 'And... what do we do now?'

Kashyap gave a small smile. 'For the time being, relax. I will come to you when the time comes. You need to get ready for the journey ahead both physically and mentally.'

'But how will we find you again?' Meenakshi inquired hurriedly.

Kashyap raised a hand, silencing her concerns.

'You need not worry. That eagle was sent by me, and you will hear from me when the time is right."'

After this, Rishi Kashyap stepped into the shiny portal behind. As the scene of him began to vanish, he hesitated, giving a final look to the remaining three.

'I will turn back time. You will not, however, dear Aarya, will not recall any of this.'

# Chapter 19

# Chronicles of the Hidden Dawn

And with that, he disappeared into the bright light of the portal.

All at once, all the objects present in the room started levitating, hovering for a while and returning back in their original positions.

The mood was different and Aarya felt an unusual conformation; blinking as though she had just woken up from a deep slumber. She knocked the door causing the hearts of that trio to quicken.

'What is the problem with all of you?' she said concerned, as if nothing had happened.

The three looked each other in extreme worry, their minds already advanced. Meenakshi was the first to remove her phone from the charger and checked the calendar; it was 16 October. They had gone a whole day backwards somehow.

'Nothing ... it is just ... nothing,' Meenakshi answered with hesitance.

But while they were still trying to digest the absurdity of what just happened, Anjali's peripheral vision noticed something lying on the window – an eagle's feather. She looked at Meenakshi and understood her without speaking.

Still seeming stupefied, Sidhant was the first one to speak.

'So ... it really was not a dream?'

Aary, not being aware of what was going on between them, chuckled.

'Dream? Which dream? And why are you holding that letter?'

The three friends completed another round of eye contact, this time more expressive. It was evident that no matter what this journey was, it had barely scratched the surface.

The weight of anguish which they bore was heavy like an ominous cloud threatening rain. Meenakshi, her hand shaking and with the letter still in her grasp, felt her breath failing her. She could already sense the heat emanating from the rest without even looking at them, their fear and bewilderment as real as hers. The pace of movement appeared to be different, the second becoming an unspeakable silence which was only drowned by the sound of trees swaying outside and the low ticking of a clock — a most irritating instrument of the time which they had lost or gained.

Anjali was the very first to look up; her bright eyes seeking for Meenakshi's as if she wanted her to understand something silently.

Resting on the cusp of the window was her hand, the point at which the eagle's feather was still moving in the window, improbable as it was. Also, she caressed her lip, her mind clouded with danger, as if she knew what she wanted to say but couldn't find the words.

Her eyes flew across to Sidhant, who was aloft looking down inside the dark reflection of the pane as if it were still day light. The playfulness that characterized him was absent from his eyes, a wary looking tension had taken over. He made a movement with his hands as if a sentence was stuck in the back of his throat but did not say anything. They were all burdened by the enormity of the events that had just taken place.

Meenakshi's heart sank and her breath hitched. She took a deep breath and her heart raced. She was also in a dilemma, how is it possible that they had traveled to the past?

How was it possible that the place which was just now a huge vortex ceiling, had suddenly reverted to being a ceiling like there was no such vortex?

A silent understanding passed among the trio as they gazed at each other again. Statements regarding the situation—specifically that it could not possibly have been a dream or a figment of the mind—remained uncommunicated by all present.

The world in which they operated had turned on its head, and they had experienced something that could not be explained or understood.

Meenakshi's grip on the letter hardened. All of them were asking themselves the same question: "What now?" yet none of them had the bravery to voice it. Not yet. They cast one last glance at one another. It was a common promise, not to give away anything until they learned more. But within that stillness, everyone sensed it — an insistent feeling that this was just the first installment of a lengthy story.

Just at that moment, Meenakshi had opened her mouth to say something when Aarya walked back in, the sound of her nonsensical footsteps resonating across the corridor like a loud bang. The trio tensed, their hearts thumping in fear, the same fear of being caught in the act of appreciating something they were forbidden to do. Aarya's merry tone cut in from nowhere, well beyond the anguished eye of the storm.

'What happened? You guys appear as if you have seen a ghost.'

Meenakshi, Sidhant and Anjali cast one last look towards each other—a look heavy with apprehension, the look of a people with a deadly secret that made them anxious about ever saying it.

No words have been exchanged, nevertheless, the strength of that silence felt together seemed to surpass any verbal communication.

www.ingramcontent.com/pod-product-compliance
Lightning Source LLC
LaVergne TN
LVHW041617070526
838199LV00052B/3183